MADRIGALS
FOR THREE
TO EIGHT VOICES

RECENT RESEARCHES IN THE MUSIC OF THE RENAISSANCE

James Haar, general editor

A-R Editions, Inc., publishes six quarterly series—

Recent Researches in the Music of the Middle Ages and Early Renaissance
Margaret Bent, general editor

Recent Researches in the Music of the Renaissance
James Haar, general editor

Recent Researches in the Music of the Baroque Era
Robert L. Marshall, general editor

Recent Researches in the Music of the Classical Era
Eugene K. Wolf, general editor

Recent Researches in the Music of the Nineteenth and Early Twentieth Centuries
Rufus Hallmark, general editor

Recent Researches in American Music
H. Wiley Hitchcock, general editor—

which make public music that is being brought to light
in the course of current musicological research.

Each volume in the *Recent Researches* is devoted
to works by a single composer or to a single genre of composition,
chosen because of its potential interest to scholars and performers,
and prepared for publication according to the standards that govern
the making of all reliable historical editions.

Subscribers to this series, as well as patrons of subscribing institutions,
are invited to apply for information about the "Copyright-Sharing Policy"
of A-R Editions, Inc., under which the contents of this volume
may be reproduced free of charge for study or performance.

Correspondence should be addressed:

A-R EDITIONS, INC.
315 West Gorham Street
Madison, Wisconsin 53703

RECENT RESEARCHES IN THE MUSIC OF THE RENAISSANCE • VOLUMES LXVI and LXVII

Stefano Rossetti

MADRIGALS FOR THREE TO EIGHT VOICES

Edited by Allen B. Skei

A-R EDITIONS, INC. • MADISON

Library of Congress Cataloging in Publication Data

Rossetti, Stefano, fl. 1560–1583.
    [Madrigals, Selections]
    Madrigals for three to eight voices.

    (Recent researches in the music of the Renaissance,
ISSN 0486–123X ; v. 66–67)
    Principally Italian words, also printed as text with
English translations on p.
    "The present edition makes available, for the first
time in score and modern notation, the twenty-nine
madrigals from Rossetti's Il primo libro de' madrigali a
sei voci and the additional three madrigals preserved only
in anthologies"—Pref.
    Bibliography: p.
    1. Madrigals (Music), Italian.   I. Skei, Allen B.
II. Rossetti, Stefano, fl. 1560–1583. Madrigals, voices
(6), book 1. 1985.   III. Series.
M2.R2384   vol. 66–67   [M1579]   84–760225
ISBN 0–89579–149–8

Contents

Preface

During a career that spanned more than twenty-five years, Stefano Rossetti (or Rossetto, as he was sometimes called) published only five books of madrigals, a book of motets, and a handful of madrigals scattered in anthologies. He also made a manuscript collection of four-voice madrigals (*Musica nova*, 1560), wrote a fifty-voice motet,[1] composed several concerted works for the Florentine carnival of 1567, and may have contributed an *intermedio* to Giovanni Fedini's *Le due Persilie* (1583).[2] Unfortunately, much of his music has since been lost, either completely or in part. All that fully survives are two published books of madrigals, the manuscript *Musica nova* of 1560, the book of motets, and three madrigals preserved in anthologies.

In addition to their musical value, Rossetti's works provide us with what little information is available regarding his life.[3] It can be briefly summarized as follows: He thought of himself as a native of Nice, where, in 1560, he made his first appearance as a composer, with the four-voice *Musica nova* written in celebration of the marriage of Emanuel Philibert of Savoy and Marguerite of Valois. The same year he was also in Schio, presumably in the employ of the Giustiani family. He subsequently became *maestro di cappella* in Novara and later, in 1564 or 1565, at the Duomo in Florence. He next turned up as organist at the Imperial Chapel in Munich, where he spent the last few months of the year 1580. Except for his contribution of an *intermedio* to a celebration in Florence in 1583, nothing more of significance is known of his life.

The present edition makes available, for the first time in score and modern notation, the twenty-nine madrigals from Rossetti's *Primo libro de' madrigali a sei voci* and the additional three madrigals preserved only in anthologies. It complements the two earlier Rossetti editions in the Recent Researches in the Music of the Renaissance series,[4] for it rounds out the modern publication of Rossetti's extant printed works—with the exception of a four-voice madrigal in two *parti* from *Musica nova* (1560) that was subsequently published in 1561.[5]

The Music

Il primo libro de' madrigali a sei voci was published in 1566 by the Venetian firm of Claudio Merulo and Fausto Bethanio. It was never reprinted, and it serves as the only source for the works it contains. Rossetti dedicated the collection to Isabella de' Medici (see Plate II), the sister of Cardinal Ferdinando de' Medici, whom Rossetti nominally served at the Duomo in Florence (the cardinal preferred to fulfill his duties from the distance of his residence in Rome). Isabella was also the wife of Duke Paolo Giordana Orsini and, in 1576, the victim of a rather bizarre murder. After dinner on the evening of 16 July, the Duke, who wanted to be free to marry his mistress, had Isabella strangled to death by a rope let down through a hole in the ceiling and held by four men above. The murder apparently took place while he was pretending to kiss her.[6]

Isabella might well have shared her family's traditional interest in the arts. Rossetti's preface to the book of 1566 refers to her as his patroness (*padrona mia*) and notes her kindness generally toward all artists (*tutti i virtuosi*). He no doubt had benefited in some way from her patronage, and in the following year he also dedicated *Il lamento di Olimpia* to her.[7]

In six partbooks, *Il primo libro de' madrigali a sei voci* contains seventeen madrigals, including eleven each in two *parti,* together with a concluding chanson, *Au joli bois.* The texts, like those set in Rossetti's *Primo libro de madregali a quattro voci* (1560), are drawn in large measure from Petrarch. Rossetti sets five of Petrarch's sonnets, a ballata, and a canzone stanza. He also sets Luigi Cassola's well-known *Altro non è il mio amor*[8] and two stanzas from Ariosto's *Orlando furioso*, from which Rossetti would also later take the text for *Il lamento di Olimpia.* Nothing is known of the authorship of the remaining texts in the collection, most of which are sonnets, beyond the fact that the poet of *Son questi quei begli occhi* must have been an admirer of Pietro Bembo's: the first two lines of the poem are identical with those of one of Bembo's sonnets.

Rossetti (or his publisher) arranges the madrigals in the collection mostly according to clef combination and key. Madrigals written in the *chiavette* precede those written in the *chiavi naturali*, and within the two groups, those in transposed modes (indicated by a signature of one flat) precede those in untransposed modes. *Au joli bois*, the only setting of a French text in the collection (and one of only three such settings in Rossetti's work altogether),[9] falls outside of the pattern; it is written in the *chiavette* and bears a signature of one flat.

Except for the use of an increased number of voices,

the collection on the whole seems rather less adventurous than Rossetti's earlier works, especially the books of four-voice madrigals from 1560, the manuscript *Musica nova* and *Il primo libro de madregali a quattro voci*. The present collection, for instance, contains no madrigals written *a note nere*, and the chromaticism, introduced here only infrequently, seems qualitatively restrained, particularly as compared to the remarkable conclusion of *Mentre che 'l cor*[10] or as compared to *Aspro cor'e selvaggia*[11] and *Vergine bella*.[12] For Rossetti, however, chromaticism continued to be an effective means of expressing the meaning of the text, as heard most notably in the opening measures of *Pieno di dolce* (No. 9) and *I dolci basci* (No. 15); yet it was a means that he seldom chose to employ in his works after 1560.

Rossetti nevertheless reveals in the present collection a continuing concern for vivid representation of the text, whether it be the battle cries of "Alla caccia! A cacciar nimphe, venite" (No. 17) or an expression of the pangs of love, as in *Se per voi sentì mai* (No. 10). He also reveals considerable concern for sonority and texture, varying both with consistent skill. Six-voice texture, of course, represents the norm within the collection, but it is a norm from which Rossetti constantly deviates in his exploration of the textural possibilities offered by the ensemble.

The publication of a book of six-voice madrigals represents a somewhat forward-looking approach for the time. Six-voice madrigals were hardly unknown in the mid-1560s, but whole books of them were certainly uncommon. Rossetti, employing a frequent and often rapid alternation of textures, takes full advantage of the six-voice ensemble. His treatment could well have been inspired, incidentally, by Philippe de Monte's first book of six-voice madrigals, the first edition of which (now lost) appeared around 1564.[13] In addition to its employment of the same alternation of vocal textures, Monte's book bears yet another resemblance to Rossetti's in its relationship to Isabella de' Medici: it contains a work written in honor of her marriage.[14]

In keeping, perhaps, with the variety of its vocal textures, Rossetti's collection also employs a frequent alternation between simple chordal motion and a number of kinds of contrapuntal movement. Variety indeed seems to be the hallmark of the collection. The collection is, however, also distinguished by an admirably clear declamation of the text and by rhythmic animation, occasionally resulting from syncopations of remarkable quality (as, for instance, in *Colmo d'ira*). Altogether, Rossetti's six-voice madrigals seem to reflect a composer of substantial skill and vivid imagination. On the basis of this collection alone, he would appear to merit consideration as fully as almost any of his contemporaries.

The three madrigals that conclude the present edition are found as *unica* in two separate published collections. *S'io non v'amo et adoro*, a setting of a canzone in seven stanzas, appears in *Il gaudio primo libro de madrigali de diversi musici a tre voci*, published in Venice by Scotto in 1586. *Quando la bella aurora*, a setting of a canzone in six stanzas and *Se dove è 'l sol*, a *dialogo a 8*, appeared in a collection edited by Giulio Bonagionta (Bonagiunta), *Gli amorosi concenti primo libro delli madrigali de diversi eccellentissimi musici*, published in Venice in 1568 by Scotto (see Plate IV).

S'io non v'amo et adoro and *Quando la bella aurora* reflect something of the rather unusual fondness shown by Rossetti for extended poetic forms. He wrote altogether seven cyclic madrigals, two each in six, seven, and eight stanzas, and one, *Fra quanti amor* (Ariosto's *Lamento di Olimpia*), in seventeen. Among them, only *Quando la bella aurora* and *Ecco pur riede*[15] conform to the normal practice of the day to retain the same number of voices for each stanza; Rossetti instead prefers to vary the number of voices, usually by increasing it gradually from stanza to stanza. In *S'io non v'amo et adoro*, however, he contents himself with presenting six stanzas *a 3* and the last stanza *a 4*. The additional voice is derived canonically from the middle voice. Proceeding at the unison, it is the only canon in Rossetti's works.

Judging from the works presented here and from the only other of his cyclic madrigals preserved in its entirety *(Ben mi credea passar)*,[16] it appears that Rossetti prefers to unify his extended works primarily by means of mode. All stanzas of *Quando la bella aurora*, for instance, end on the modal final, G. In *S'io non v'amo et adoro*, he simply pairs the first two and last two stanzas: the first and sixth stanzas end on A and the second and seventh on the final, D. Such pairing appears to be rather common in the cyclic madrigal generally.

The authors of the two lengthy *canzoni*, *Quando la bella aurora* and *S'io non v'amo et adoro*, are unknown. It seems clear only that the poet of the latter was neither a polished nor an experienced writer. The poem itself seems rather crudely made, and it concludes with the hope—which might well be shared by some of its readers—that the poet would never have to write another: *Io credo che bastar tu debbi sola, / canzon, ad apportarmi pace o triegua / nè mi sia huopo ch'un'altra ne segua.*

Se dove è 'l sol, which closes the collection *Gli amorosi concenti*, is a setting of an anonymous ballata for two groups of four voices each. Rossetti's designation of the work as a *dialogo* implies only an alternation between groups and not an interchange between characters or speakers within a poem. Dramatic dialogues were well known in the sixteenth century but probably no more well known than the antiphonal presentation of a single poetic voice, as is the case here.[17] Rossetti's adoption of the form may have been inspired by the dialogues in Florentine *intermedii* of his day.

The Edition

The notation in the original publications poses no particular problems. Duple meter appears only with the signature *tempus imperfectum diminutum* (¢), which is transcribed here with the signature $\frac{2}{2}$; triple meter is usually introduced with the signature **C3**, which is transcribed with the signature $\frac{6}{8}$. Blackened notation is also employed in the source to produce triple meter (as in *Come va 'l mondo!*, mm. 8–9) and for the purpose of creating eye-music as well (e.g., for "l'ombra" in *Quando la bella aurora*, last stanza, m. 32). Blackened notation is indicated in the edition by broken horizontal brackets and, where appropriate, triplet signs.

The compositions are presented here in open score with the original note values halved. At the beginning of each piece, each line of the score has an incipit that presents a quotation of the original clef and signatures and the range of the part in transcription.

Except for the occasional regularization of spellings among voice parts, the original spellings of the texts are retained throughout these volumes. Modernized capitalization, diacritical marks, and punctuation have been supplied by the editor. In the Texts and Translations section and in the titles for the madrigals, some of the elisions that occur in the underlaid texts of the sources and edition have been expanded. This has been done in order to have the printed texts reflect the standard poetic form. In the original publications, repetitions of text are often indicated only by the abbreviation *ij*. Text in the present edition that has been supplied for such indications is enclosed in angled brackets; other additions are enclosed in square brackets.

In the original editions, accidentals are valid for the note that follows the symbol and for each successive note of the same pitch; a rest or a note of different pitch generally cancels the previous accidental. Except for the use of sharps to cancel flats (including flats required by the signature), Rossetti and his contemporaries employed no other means for cancellations. All cancellations of accidentals in the present edition have, therefore, been supplied by the editor through the use of barlines or by means of accidentals placed, like all editorial inflections, above the staff. In the edition, when successive altered notes fall in two or more measures, the accidental is repeated at the beginning of each new measure without special designation or comment.

Notes on Performance

The music should move as quickly as the meaning of the text allows but not so quickly that the words and contrapuntal lines are obscured. The metronome marking ♩ = 80 can often be used as a starting point. Since absolute pitch was generally unknown in the six-teenth century, the users of the present edition should feel free to transpose any of the pieces as needed to fit the ranges of the voices at hand.

Ideally, Rossetti's madrigals—like other madrigals from the period—should be performed with one singer on each part. Instruments can occasionally be substituted for voices, especially when an insufficient number of singers is available.

Also ideally, the madrigals in two or more parts should be performed in full. The Petrarchan sonnet, with its characteristic change in tone and direction at the beginning of the last six lines, may indeed lend itself to a setting in two musically independent parts, but the text in each part usually depends so much on the other that it makes little or incomplete sense alone. Canzone stanzas, however, can often stand alone and, in their musical settings, be performed alone.

Critical Notes

The original publications are relatively free of error. The following notes detail the few errors that there are; the notes also indicate aspects of the original notation not seen in the present edition. The original readings are listed below by the number of the work in question. Pitch designations are of the usual sort: middle C is c', the C an octave higher is c", and so forth. Abbreviations are as follows: M = measure; C = canto; A = alto; Q = quinto; T = tenor; S = sesto; and B = basso.

No. 5—M. 8–m. 9, note 2, C, A, S, B have blackened semibreves and minims.

No. 12— A and S partbooks omit the designation *se-conda parte*, which appears in the other partbooks possibly by mistake—the poems of Nos. 11 and 12 are un-related in form and only slightly related in content.

No. 14—Mm. 6–7, all parts, text is "pruio," almost certainly a misprint for *privo*. Mm. 7–8 and 10, all parts, text is "Il vostr'Autume," which is probably a misread-ing for *Il vostr'autore*.

No. 16—Mm. 15–16, T, text is "vedend'agghiac-ciar."

No. 17—Mm. 4–8, only the A reads "fornite forti," garbling the text; the other parts read "finite forte" and "fenite forti."

No. 22—M. 56, A, note 5 is a'.

Nos. 28 and 29—in A partbook the order and num-bering are reversed.

No. 30—*Prima stanza*: M. 39, T, note 3 is a semi-minim. *Sesta stanza*: M. 41, C, minim and dotted semi-breve (c", d") inserted after first beat. M. 49, C, note 2 is sharped. M. 50, C, note is b'. *Settima & ultima stanza*: T part bears the instruction *canon in unitate* together with the appropriate indications for beginning and ending the canon. M. 4, C, last note sharped in original; sharp may be a cautionary sign, indicating that *musica ficta* should not be applied, or it may simply be an error.

No. 31—*Quarta stanza:* M. 4, T, note 4 omitted. *Sesta & ultima stanza:* M. 32, A, note 2 is a fusa.

Acknowledgments

A complete copy of *Il primo libro de' madrigali a sei voci* is preserved in the British Library, a copy of *Il gaudio primo libro de madrigali* in the Deutsche Staatsbibliothek, Berlin, and a copy of *Gli amorosi concenti* in the Henry E. Huntington Library (San Marino, California). I am indebted to these libraries for supplying the microfilm and electrostatic copies from which this edition was prepared. I am all the more indebted to the British Library and the Henry E. Huntington Library for permission to reproduce here pages from the original publications. For initial assistance with the texts in the edition, I am grateful to Professor Cecil Grayson (Oxford University) and to Loretta Cousins (Eureka, California), and for subsequent assistance to Professor Maurice Gendron (California State University, Fresno) and especially Professor Ruggero Stefanini (University of California, Berkeley). I am also indebted to my colleague Professor Paul Kinzel for his translation of *Au joli bois*. The debt to my colleague Professor Adriana Slaniceanu is largest of all, not only for her translations of many of the texts but also for the quality of the literary insights she provided.

My thanks go also to Harvard University Press for permission to quote Robert M. Durling's fine translations of Petrarch, to Oxford University Press for permission to quote Guido Waldman's translation of *Orlando furioso*, and to *The Music Review* and its editor A. F. Leighton Thomas for permission to reprint portions of an article of mine that appears in that journal ("Stefano Rossetti, Madrigalist," vol. 39, no. 2).

Finally, financial assistance for the preparation of the edition was generously given by California State University, Fresno. I appreciate the support.

Allen B. Skei

Notes

1. *Consolamini, consolamini, popule meus,* Mus. MS. 1536, Maier No. 132, Bayerische Staatsbibliothek (Munich). Eighteen of the fifty parts are lost.

2. Nino Pirrotta and Elena Povoledo, *Music and Theatre from Poliziano to Monteverdi,* trans. Karen Eales (Cambridge: Cambridge University Press, 1982), 197, 206.

3. For a discussion of his music generally and for a more detailed account of his life, see Allen B. Skei, "Stefano Rossetti, Madrigalist," *The Music Review* 39 (1978): 81–94.

4. Stefano Rossetti, *Sacrae cantiones,* ed. Allen B. Skei, Recent Researches in the Music of the Renaissance, vol. 15 (Madison, Wis.: A-R Editions, 1973); Stefano Rossetti, *Il primo libro de madregali a quattro voci,* ed. Allen B. Skei, Recent Researches in the Music of the Renaissance, vol. 26 (Madison, Wis.: A-R Editions, 1977).

5. *Quel lume da cui il ciel* and *Quante eccelenze de le cose belle,* in *Madregali di Verdelot a sei insieme altri madregali di diversi eccellentissimi autori* (Venice: A. Gardano, 1561).

6. For a fuller account of the murder and the circumstances surrounding it, see Christopher Hibbert, *The House of Medici: Its Rise and Fall* (New York: Morrow, 1975), 277–78. Also see Marcel Brion, *The Medici: A Great Florentine Family,* trans. Gilles and Heather Cremonesi (London: Elek, 1969), 197, which reproduces a portrait of Isabella as stamped on a medal from 1560.

7. Stefano Rossetti, *Il lamento di Olimpia* (Venice: Scotto, 1567).

8. For a general discussion of the poem and its musical settings, see James Haar, "*Altro non è 'l mio amor,*" in *Words and Music: The Scholar's View,* ed. Laurence Berman (Cambridge, Mass.: Harvard University, Department of Music, 1972), 93–114.

9. The two additional chansons also appeared in 1566, in *Musica nova del Rossetto a cinque voci,* published in Rome by Dorico.

10. From *Il primo libro de madregali a quattro voci.*

11. From *Musica nova* (1560).

12. Ibid.

13. Alfred Einstein, *The Italian Madrigal,* trans. Alexander H. Krappe, Roger H. Sessions, and Oliver Strunk, rev. ed. (Princeton, N.J.: Princeton University Press, 1971), 2:506.

14. Ibid. Einstein suggests that the book might originally have been dedicated to her husband.

15. The latter madrigal is from *Terzo libro del desiderio. Madrigali a quattro voci di Orlando Lasso et d'altri eccel. musici,* ed. Giulio Bonagionta (Venice: Scotto, 1567).

16. From *Musica nova* (1560).

17. David Nutter and John Whenham, "Dialogue," *The New Grove Dictionary of Music and Musicians,* ed. Stanley Sadie (London: Macmillan, 1980), 5:415–17.

Texts and Translations

Nos. 1 and 2—Petrarch, Sonnet, 213

1. Gratie ch'a pochi il ciel largo destina,
   Rara virtù, non già d'humana gente,
   Sotto biondi capei canuta mente,
   E 'n humil donna alta beltà divina;

   Leggiadria singulare et pellegrina,
   E 'l cantar che ne l'anima si sente,
   L'andar celeste e 'l vago spirto ardente
   Ch'ogni dur rompe et ogni altezza inchina;

2. Et quei begli occhi che i cor fanno smalti,
   Possenti a rischiarar abisso et notti,
   Et torre l'alme a' corpi et darle altrui;

   Col dir pien d'intelletti dolci et alti,
   Coi sospiri soavemente rotti:
   Da questi magi trasformato fui.

(Graces that generous Heaven allots to few, virtues rare beyond the custom of men, beneath blond hair the wisdom of gray age, and in a humble lady high divine beauty,
   singular, strange charm and singing that is felt in the soul, a heavenly walk and a lovely ardent spirit that breaks all that is hard and makes every height bow down,

   and those lovely eyes that turn hearts to stone, powerful enough to brighten the abyss and night and to take souls from their bodies and give them to others,
   with speech full of sweet high insights, and sighs sweetly broken—by these magicians was I transformed.)

Translation by Robert M. Durling.[1]

Nos. 3 and 4—Petrarch, Sonnet, 269

3. Rotta è l'alta colonna e 'l verde lauro
   Che facean ombra al mio stanco pensero:
   Perduto ho quel che ritrovar non spero
   Dal borea a l'austro o dal mar indo al mauro.

   Tolto m'hai, morte, il mio doppio thesauro
   Che mi fea viver lieto et gire altero,
   E ristorar nol po terra nè impero,
   Nè gemma oriental nè forza d'auro.

4. Ma se consentimento è di destino,
   Che posso io più se no haver l'alma trista,
   Humidi gli occhi sempre e 'l viso chino?

   O nostra vita ch'è sì bella 'n vista,
   Com' perde agevolmente in un mattino
   Quel che 'n molti anni a gran pena s'acquista!

(Broken are the high Column and the green Laurel that gave shade to my weary cares; I have lost what I do not hope to find again, from Boreas to Auster or from the Indian to the Moorish Sea.
   You have taken from me, O Death, my double treasure that made me live glad and walk proudly; neither land nor empire can restore it, nor orient gem, nor the power of gold.

   But, since this is the intent of destiny, what can I do except have my soul sad, my eyes always wet, and my face bent down?
   Oh our life that is so beautiful to see, how easily it loses in one morning what has been acquired with great difficulty over many years!)

Translation by Robert M. Durling.

Nos. 5 and 6—Petrarch, Sonnet, 290

5. Come va 'l mondo! hor mi diletta et piace
   Quel che più mi dispiacque, hor veggio et sento
   Che per haver salute hebbi tormento
   Et breve guerra per eterna pace.

   O speranza, o desir sempre fallace
   E degli amanti più ben per un cento!
   O quant'era il peggior farmi contento
   Quella ch'or siede in cielo e 'n terra giace!

6. Ma 'l cieco Amor e la mia sorda mente
   Mi traviavan sì ch'andar per viva
   Forza mi convenia dove morte era:

   Benedetta colei ch'a miglior riva
   Volse il mio corso et l'empia voglia ardente
   Lusingando affrenò perch'io non pera!

(How the world goes! now I am pleased and delighted by what most displeased me, now I see and feel that in order to have salvation I had torment, and brief war for eternal peace.
   Oh hope, oh desire, always deceptive and for lovers more so by a hundred times! Oh how much worse it would have been if she had contented me, who is now enthroned in Heaven and lies in earth!

   But blind Love and my deaf mind led me so astray that by their lively force I had to go where Death was;
   blessed be she who turned my course toward a better shore and, alluring my wicked ardent will, reined it in that I might not perish!)

Translation by Robert M. Durling.

7. Son questi quei begli occhi in cui mirando
   Senza diffesa far perdei me stesso.
   È questo il fronte dove Amor vien spesso,
   Le faci e le saette indi tirando.

   È questo il crin ch'all'aura sventilando
   Veddo andar io hor sì celato e presso,
   Sta sotto un vel leggiadramente messo,
   Per cui tanti sospir in vano spando.

8. Ahi! Chi sarà colui che più si fidi
   Di fè di donna mobile e inconstante?
   E chi più a femminil pianto mai creda?

   Veggendo a miei desir constanti e fidi,
   Questa Fedra crudel volger le piante
   E cercar empia un'altra nuova preda.

(These are those lovely eyes, the beholding of which made me, who was without defense, lose myself. This is the battlefront to which Love often comes, shooting torches and arrows.

These are the tresses that were blowing in the breeze that I now see hidden nearby, worn gracefully under a veil. These are the tresses for which I in vain pour forth so many sighs.

Oh, who can be the one who still trusts in the faith of changeable and inconstant woman? And who can still believe feminine tears?

Seeing my constant and faithful desires, this cruel Phaedra turns her back and wickedly seeks another prey.)

Translation by Adriana Slaniceanu.

9. Pieno di dolce et d'amoroso effetto,
   Alla sua sonna, a la sua diva corse,
   Che con le braccia al collo il tennea stretto,
   Quel ch'al Cattai non havria fatto forse.
   Al patrio regno, al suo natio ricetto,
   Seco havendo costui, l'animo torse:
   Subito in lei s'aviva la speranza
   Di tosto riveder sua riccha stanza.

(Brimful of gentle, loving thoughts he ran to his lady, his goddess, who threw her arms tightly about his neck—which she would perhaps not have done in her native Cathay. Now that she had his company, her thoughts turned to her father's kingdom, the cradle of her birth; hope suddenly revived in her of soon regaining her precious home.)

Translation by Guido Waldman.[2]

10. Se per voi sentì mai fiamma d'amore
    Questo corpo dolente afflitto e lasso,
    Hor arso 'l petto et infiammato 'l core
    Si sente e ne diventa immobil sasso.

Et è condotto a tal che qua si muore
Da gli spiriti vital privato e casso
De l'usato sostegno, et se l'aita
Hora non fia, sento mancar mia vita.

(If a lover ever felt for you, this aching, vexed, and tired body now feels, the breast burning and the heart inflamed, and turns into an immovable stone. And it is brought to the point where it dies, deprived of the breath of life and devoid of its usual sustenance. And now that there be no help, I feel my life pass away.)

Translation by Adriana Slaniceanu.

11. Io me ne vo la notte (Amore è duce)
    A ritrovar la bella Fiordispina;
    E v'arrivai che non era la luce
    Del sole ascosa ancor ne la marina.
    Beato è chi correndo si conduce
    Prima degli a dir a la reina,
    Da lei sperando per l'anuntio buono
    Acquistar gratia e riportarne dono.

12. Felice me se de bei lumi un raggio,
    Che di viltà mi spoglia,
    In mio favor s'unisse con la voglia.
    Servendo havete a cui par non ha 'l mondo
    In questo mortal velo.
    Non fora al mio bello stato secondo
    Se non ch'i' viva in cielo.
    Ma ahimè! Che mi si muove un gelo
    E temo non mi toglia
    Il cor di quel che l'occhio più m'invoglia.

(I set off by night, with Cupid for guide, to be with lovely Fiordispina, and I arrived before the Sun had hidden his radiance in the sea. Happy the man who outstripped his fellows in bringing the news to the princess: as bearer of good tidings he could expect thanks and a reward from her.

Happy were I if a ray of beautiful light, which would strip me of cowardice, would—for my benefit—be united with my desire. You have served the one who has no equal in this world, under this mortal veil. I would not be in my beautiful second state were I not living in paradise. But alas! An icy feeling moves me, and I am afraid not to free myself from the heart of the one who most attracts my eyes.)

Translation of No. 11 by Guido Waldman.
Translation of No. 12 by Adriana Slaniceanu.

13. Donna bella e gentil ch'al ciel poggiate
    Con la figlia sovente di Latona,
    Onde Giove di voi sì vago fate,
    Che mai sempre a mirarvi Amor lo sprona.

L'altro hier per mirar voi havea lasciato
Le Dee celesti il scettro e la corona
E quagiù in mortal forma, ricercate
Tutte l'alme contrade di Cremona.

14. Colmo d'ira e di sdegno al fin vi scorse
Girar chiuso in un carro onde e i fè privo,
Il vostro autore, don d'ingegno e d'arte,
Di ciò per voi ciascun mostrossi schivo.
Ma ben a Giove caldi voti porse
Perchè spezzasse 'l carro a parte a parte.

(Beautiful and gentle lady, who often ascends to heaven with Latona's daughter, you thereby create in Jove such longing that Love incites him to look at you constantly.

The other day, in order to look at you, he abandoned the celestial goddesses, scepter, and crown, and here below, in mortal form, searched all of Cremona's fertile countryside.

Full of anger and wrath, he at last found you traveling shut up in a carriage, which took his hopes away. Your father, a master of ingenuity and art, made everyone restrain himself for your sake, but he offered fervent prayers to Jove that he would break the carriage to pieces.)

Translation by Adriana Slaniceanu.

Nos. 15 and 16—Unidentified, Sonnet

15. I dolci basci sì soavi e cari,
I desiati e dolci abbracciamenti,
E le dolce accoglienze e i dolci accenti
Con dolci modi espressi unici e rari.

E quei soavi dolci pianti amari,
I profondo sospir, dolci e cocenti
E gli dolci commun ragionamenti
Ch'arder con dolci modi fa ch'impari.

16. M'hanno condotto a tal ch'io non ho possa
E credendo agghiacciar ardo nel fuoco
Che così vuol chi può di me che vuole

Perchè non mi fu stata una sol cosa,
Concessa nel oscuro e dolce luoco
C'havesse 'l suo camin tardato 'l sole?

(The sweet kisses so gentle and dear, the longed-for and tender embraces, and the sweet welcome, the sweet accents, with sweet ways expressed uniquely and rarely,

and those soft, bittersweet tears, the deepest sighs, sweet and burning, and the sweet, common reasonings that shine with charming manner, that make me learn—

they have led me to where I have no power, to where I think I'm freezing when I burn with fire, to the point—as she wants—where she can do with me whatever she wishes.

Why was I not granted just one thing, that the sun might have delayed its arrival in that sweet dark place?)

Translation by Adriana Slaniceanu.

Nos. 17 and 18—Unidentified, Sonnet

17. Alla caccia! A cacciar nimphe, venite.
Fornite forti di bon armatura
Et archi e frezze sien di tempra dura,
Rigidose rugendo inscieme unite.

Di fuori di pietà siate vestite,
Indegnate in colui che pon gran cura
Noi nimphe nichilar e far paura
Apportandoci a noi l'antica lite.

18. Noia non vi serà, dunque, se dite
D'essere di Diana fide serve,
Oprare ogni arte con giusta ragione.

Mettetevi in battaglia e ben ardite,
Errando andate per di qui proterve,
Desiderose di farlo prigione.

(To the hunt! To the hunt, you nymphs, come all, strongly outfitted with good armor and bows and arrows of hard temper, united together with an unrelenting roar.

Outwardly be cloaked in compassion but contemptuous of the one who is trying so hard to annihilate and frighten us, bringing to us the ancient quarrel.

It will not vex you, then, to say you are Diana's faithful servants, and to practice each art with good reason.

Plunge into battle and, with great daring, rove about arrogantly, anxious to take him [Amore] prisoner.[3])

Translation by Adriana Slaniceanu.

No. 19—Luigi Cassola, Madrigal

19. Altro non è il mio amor ch'il proprio inferno
Perchè l'inferno è sol vedersi privo
Di contemplar nel ciel un sol Dio vivo,
Nè altro duol non v'è nel fuoco eterno.
Adunque il proprio inferno è l'amor mio
Ch'in tutto privo di veder son'io
Quel dolce ben, che sol veder desio.
Ahi! Possanza d'Amor quanto sei forte
Che fai gustar l'inferno anti la morte.

(My love is nothing other than hell itself, for hell is to see oneself unable to contemplate in heaven the one living God; there is no other pain within the eternal fire. Therefore, my own love is hell itself, for I am entirely deprived of the sight of that sweet goodness which alone I wish to see. Ah, how strong is the power of Love to make us taste hell before death!)

Translation by Adriana Slaniceanu.

20. S'io potessi mirar quell'occhi belli
   Senza la tema di maggior mio danno,
   O, che felice amor, che dolce affanno.
   Ma la fortuna adversa a miei desiri,
   Et la mia fera stella
   Della mia donna bella
   M'allontana in guisa ch'i sospiri
   Crescano ogn'hor più forte
   Tal ch'io bramo che morte
   In li miei più verdi anni
   Ponga omai fine a così lunghi affanni.

(If I could behold those lovely eyes without fear of increased harm to myself, oh, what happy love, what sweet anguish! But fortune is unfavorable to my desires, and the cruel star of my beautiful lady sends me away so that my sighs grow stronger each hour. Thus, in my greenest years, I long for death to put an end to such lasting anguish.)

Translation by Adriana Slaniceanu.

Nos. 21 and 22—Petrarch, Sonnet, 321

21. È questo 'l nido in che la mia phenice
   Mise l'aurate et le purpuree penne?
   Che sotto le sue ali il mio cor tenne,
   Et parole et sospiri anco n'elice?

   O del dolce mio mal prima radice,
   Ov'è il bel viso onde quel lume venne
   Che vivo et lieto ardendo mi mantenne?
   Sol'eri in terra; hor sei nel ciel felice,

22. Et m'hai lasciato qui misero e solo,
   Tal che pien di duol sempre al luoco torno
   Che per te consecrato honoro et colo,

   Veggendo a' colli oscura notte intorno
   Onde prendesti al ciel l'ultimo volo
   Et dove gli occhi tuoi solean far giorno.

(Is this the nest where my phoenix put on her gold and purple feathers, where she kept my heart beneath her wings and still wrings from it words and sighs?

O first root of my sweet harms, where is the lovely face whence came the light that kept me alive and glad though burning? You were unique on earth, now you are happy in Heaven,

and you have left me here wretched and alone, so that full of grief I return always to the place that I honor and adore as consecrated to you,

seeing dark night around the hills whence you took your last flight to Heaven and where your eyes used to make day.)

Translation by Robert M. Durling.

No. 23—Petrarch, Rime disperse, Ballata

23. Nova bellezza in habito gentile
   Volse il mio core a l'amorosa schiera
   Ove 'l mal si sostene e 'l ben si spera.

   Gir mi convene e star, com'altri vole,
   Poi ch'al vago pensier fu posto un freno
   Di dolci sdegni e di pietosi sguardi,
   E 'l chiaro nome e 'l suon de le parole
   De la mia donna e 'l bel viso sereno
   Son le faville, Amor, perchè 'l cor m'ardi.
   Io pur spero, quantunque che sia tardi,
   Che avenga ella si mostre acerba e fiera,
   Humile amante vince donna altiera.

(New beauty in a noble habit turned my heart to the amorous flock where pain is suffered and good is hoped for.

I must go and stand still at another's will, since on my wandering thoughts has been placed a bridle of sweet scorns and merciful glances; and the bright name and the sound of the words of my lady, and her clear face are the sparks, Love, with which you burn my heart.

I still hope, however late it might be, for, though she happen to be bitter and fierce, a humble lover overcomes a proud lady.)

Translation adapted from Robert M. Durling.[4]

No. 24—Petrarch, Canzone, 332

24. Nessun visse già mai più di me lieto,
   Nessun vive più tristo et giorni et notti,
   Et doppiando 'l dolor, doppia lo stile,
   Che trahe del cor sì lacrimose rime.
   Vissi di speme, hor vivo pur di pianto,
   Nè contra Morte spero altro che morte.

(No one ever lived more glad than I,
no one lives more sorrowful both day and night
or, sorrow doubling, redoubles his style
that draws from his heart such tearful rhymes.
I lived on hope, now I live only on weeping,
nor against Death do I hope for anything but death.)

Translation by Robert M. Durling.

Nos. 25 and 26—Petrarch, Sonnet, 223

25. Quando 'l sol bagna in mar l'aurato carro
   Et l'aere nostro et la mia mente imbruna,
   Col cielo et con le stelle et con la luna
   Un'angosciosa et dura notte innarro;

   Poi, lasso, a tal che non m'ascolta narro
   Tutte le mie fatiche ad una ad una,
   Et col mondo et con mia cieca fortuna,
   Con Amor, con Madonna et meco garro.

26. Il sonno è 'n bando, et del risposo è nulla;
   Ma sospiri et lamenti infin al l'alba
   Et lagrime che l'alma a gli occhi invia.

   Vien poi l'aurora et l'aura fosca inalba,
   Me no: ma 'l sol che 'l cor m'arde et trastulla,
   Quel può sol addolcir la doglia mia.

(When the sun bathes in the sea his gilded chariot and darkens our air and my mind, with the heavens and with the stars and with the moon I begin an anguished, bitter night;

then, alas, to one who does not listen I tell all my troubles one by one, and I quarrel with the world and with my blind fortune, with Love, with my lady, and with myself.

Sleep is banished and there is no rest, but sighs and laments till dawn, and tears that the soul sends forth to the eyes.

Then the dawn comes and lights up the dark air, but not me; the sun that burns and delights my heart, only that one can sweeten my suffering.)

Translation by Robert M. Durling.

Nos. 27 and 28—Unidentified, Sonnet

27. La pianta che tanti anni coi bei fiori
   L'Italia anzi l'Europa havea illustrato,
   E col soave odor il santo prato
   Alzata a gloria, fama, trionfi, honori,

   Gran tempo e già che non mandava fuori
   Col purpureo color germoglio ornato
   È l'alma sposa di tal ben privato
   Ch'a pietà move del suo stato i cori.

28. Ma, ecco in questa dolce primavera
   (Mercè del pio pastor) rosa gentile
   Fuor de la buccia sparte allegra altiera.

   Valor, animo invito in atto humile
   Porta el rosso mantel, gioioso spera
   Far suo nome volar dal Batra al Thile.

(The plant that with its beautiful flowers has so long reflected glory upon Italy as well as Europe has, with its sweet aroma, lifted up the hallowed meadows to glory, fame, triumphs, and honors.

It has been a long time now since she has sent out a bud adorned with crimson color. The beloved bride, deprived of such a good, moves hearts to pity by her condition.

But here in this sweet spring (thanks to the pious shepherd) a gentle rose breaks from its bud happy and proud.

Courage, the indomitable soul—in a modest gesture—wears the red mantle, and joyously hopes to make its name spread from Batra [Lower Egypt] to Thule.)

Translation by Adriana Slaniceanu.

No. 29—Unidentified, Chanson

29. Au joli bois sur le verdure,
   De mon ami je suis trompée.
   De n'avoir regret je n'ai cure
   De lui suis bien recompansée.
   Car pour abbattre la rousée,
   En lui faisant le joli seubresault,
   Il est galant quant le bon vin point ne lui fault.

(In the pretty grove, on the green grass,
I was wrong in not being filled with regret
for not having cared for my sweetheart,
although I have been rewarded.
In order to stop blushing,
I gave him a playful shove,
for he is very affectionate when he has had enough
   wine.)

Translation by Paul Kinzel.

No. 30—Unidentified, Canzone

30. Prima stanza
   S'io non v'amo et adoro,
   E se voi non tenete in mano la chiave
   De la mia libertade e del mio core,
   Giamai scemi l'ardore,
   Onde io mi strugo volontario e moro
   Nè sia più l'ardore mio dolce e soave.
   Et quel che sia più grave
   A voi del languir mio, Donna non caglie,
   Nè altra che voi vaglie
   Scemar parte del duol che mi tormenta.
   Nè l'angeliche notti ascolti o senta,
   Nè veder possa quei celesti lumi
   Che fan' de gli occhi altrui fontane e fiumi.

Seconda stanza
   Ma sì com'è pur vero,
   E come in sì gran tempo a prove tante,
   Vi potesti chiarir quella voi sete
   Che di quest'alma havete
   Quel fermo regno e quel sì fido impero,
   Di che non sia giamai ch'alma si vante.
   E se più fido amante,
   Da che 'l fuoco fu caldo e freddo 'l gelo,
   Di me non vide 'l cielo
   Perchè 'l guardo leggiadro ov'è raccolto,
   Quanto di vago ha 'l mondo, hoimè, mi è tolto,
   E perchè privo son, senza ch'io errassi,
   Di quei begli occhi ove mia vita stassi.

Terza stanza

Se quando voi tal'hora
Ver' me volgete, in cortese atto e pio,
Gli occhi, o sia a caso, o che di me vi doglia,
In fronte ogni sua voglia
Il cor vi scopre e vi dimostra all'hora.
E ciò ch'in se rinchiude 'l pensier mio,
Come nel volto a Dio
Veggon l'alme là su palese e sculto
Ogni secreto occulto.
Perchè a publico inganno e a vano sospetto
Date certa credenza e vero ricetto,
E perchè più di quel che'l vostro vede,
Voi dar' dovete ad un'altro occhio fede.

Quarta stanza

Il bel ch'in voi risplende
Non è tal, o mio sol, che sol si brami;
Mentre l'occhio vi scorge e poi s'oblia
Nè d'huom che vostro sia
Amor tal cura e così poca prende
Che lo lasci in poter perchè un'altra ami.
Son fiamme e reti et ami
Gli sguardi e le parole il riso e l'opre.
E ciò ch'in voi si scuopre,
Si che pur che ve mira una sol volta,
Non sia mai che sen vadi anima sciolta;
Così presso e lontan forzate i cuori
Che convien' ch'ogni un v'ami, ogni un v'adori.

Quinta stanza

Chi non sà come impiaghi
Lo strale d'Amor nè come 'l laccio prenda
Le più dure e sciolte alme ogn'hor fra noi
Gli occhi rivolge in voi
E guarda il volto e gli atti honesti e vaghi.
E 'l dolce suon delle parole intenda
Ch'all'hor quanto egli offenda
E quanto seco 'l contradir sia vano.
Vedrasi chiaro e piano
Che gli parrà ch'al terzo non ariva
Ciò che nè parla 'l mondo tutto e scrive;
Io 'l so, che'l suo valor temea sì poco
Pria che tocco m'havesse 'l vostro foco.

Sesta stanza

Se quando il vago aspetto
De l'antica Romana il cor gli accese
Visto havesse Tarquino i vostri rai,
Lucretia aperto mai
Non s'havrebbe col ferro il casto petto,
Nè perduto 'l suo regno e i che l'offese.
Perchè il girar cortese
De' bei vostri occhi e 'l guardo novo e
Santo tal forza stato e tanto
C'havria non sol dall'infiamata mente
Trataglia a forza ogn'altra cura ardente,
Ma spento ancor la così voglia ardita
Ch'a lui tolse l'imperio a lei la vita.

Settima & ultima stanza

Io credo che bastar tu debbi sola,
Canzon, ad apportarmi pace o triegua
Nè mi sia huopo ch'un'altra ne segua.

(If I do not love and adore you, and if in your hand you do not hold the key to my freedom and my heart, may the heat never diminish from which I willingly melt and die. May my warmth from it be more sweet and gentle; and what may be to you my gravest languishing, lady, do not quell. Nor is anyone but you able to diminish a part of the pain that torments me. I neither hear nor notice the angelic nights, nor am I able to see those celestial lights which make fountains and rivers out of the eyes of others.

But as it is indeed true, and has been true for such a long time with so many proofs, you could convince yourself that you are the one who has firm reign over this soul and faithful empire, about which may the soul never boast. And if a more faithful lover than I has heaven seen since fire was hot and ice was cold, it is because the lovely face in which is contained all the beauty the world possesses is, alas, taken from me and because I am deprived, through no fault of my own, of those beautiful eyes in which my life resides.

When, in kind and charitable gesture, you sometimes turn your eyes to me, either by chance or because you feel pity for me, my heart, contrary to any wish of its own, exposes and reveals itself to you. And what is locked up in my thoughts, as in God's face, the souls above see manifest and clear, even every hidden secret. Since to public deception and to vain suspicion you give sure faith and true refuge, and because there is more than what your eyes can see, you must place your trust in another's eyes.

The beauty aglow in you is not such, o my sun, that one only longs for it. While the eye notices you and then forgets, Love does not take such little care of the man who is yours as to leave him with the power to love another. Your looks and words, your smiles and gestures, are flames and nets and bait. And what one discovers in you, even if he looks at you only once, one never discovers without the soul freely following. So near and so far do you place hearts under compulsion that it is necessary for everyone to love you, for everyone to adore you.

He who does not know how Love's arrow hurts nor how the bond fetters the most hardened and freest souls still among us, directs his eyes toward you and looks at your face and at your honest and beautiful acts. Let him understand the sweet sound of words, which, no matter how much he assails them, it is for him useless to contradict. It will be seen clearly and plainly that he does not understand a third of what the world speaks and writes. I do know it, I who feared its force so little before your fire touched me.

If Tarquinus had seen your rays when the lovely appearance of the ancient Roman woman fired his heart, Lucretia would never have opened her chaste breast with a sword, nor would he who offended her have lost his reign, for the kind movement of your beautiful eyes and your fresh and godly face would have been such that they would not only have snatched away every burning care from his inflamed mind but would even have wiped out the bold desire that took away his empire and her life.

I believe that you alone must suffice, my song, to bring me peace and respite and that there will be no need for me to follow it up with another.)

Translation by Adriana Slaniceanu.

No. 31—Unidentified, Canzone

31. Prima stanza

Quando la bella aurora inanzi al sole
Sgombra le nebbie de l'humida notte,
I pargoletti augelli in selve e in boschi,
Quali sfogando amore e quali il pianto,
In dolci accenti et in soavi note
Surgon tra rami salutando l'alba.

Seconda stanza

Lasso che come veggio aprir a l'alba
L'uscio de l'Oriente e alletta il sole,
Io ricomincio in dolorose note,
Chiamando ogn'hora la passata notte,
Stilar per gli occhi un doloroso pianto
Tal che fo risentir le selve e i boschi.

Terza stanza

Così noiando io vo le selve e i boschi
E dico: "Invidiosa e fiera l'alba,
Che mi toglie alla gioia e dammi al pianto
Con l'aprir il sentier sì tosto al sole,
E sottrammi sì dolce e cara notte,
Cagion ch'io spargo al ciel sì fiere note."

Quarta stanza

All'hor che cantan poi gli augei lor canto
E che veggio coprir d'intorno i boschi
Dal fosco e nero velo de la notte,
E che dal nostro ciel partendo l'alba
Seco ne mena a l'altra gente il sole
In un lieto cantar rivolgo il pianto.

Quinta stanza

Così in lieto cantar il tristo pianto
Converto e i mesti accenti in dolci note,
Così, come animal che sdegna il sole,
Gode de l'ombra nei solinghi boschi,
E sol bramo e desio che giamai l'alba,
Con l'apportar del dì, scacci la notte.

Sesta & ultima stanza

Madonna, al mio languir venne una notte
In sogno e con la mano asciugò 'l pianto

Che versavan questi occhi a notte e ad alba.
E disse ben fia tempo in chiare note,
"Che non sarai più cittadin de boschi,"
Poi fuggì via sì come l'ombra al sole.

(When the beautiful dawn, in the presence of the sun, vanquishes the damp night's mists, the tiny birds in woods and forests—some giving vent to love and some to crying—spring forth through the branches greeting the dawn in sweet accents and gentle tones.

Weary as I see the Orient's door opening at dawn to entice the sun, I begin once more with dolorous tones, always recalling the night past, letting flow from my eyes such painful tears that I cause the woods and forests to resound.

So I keep on disturbing the woods and forests and say: "Envious and cruel dawn, who takes me away from joy and gives me over to tears, you steal such a sweet, precious night by making way so early for the sun. That is why I send forth such harsh tones to the sky."

Then, when the birds sing their song and I see the forest covered all around by night's gloomy black veil and that the dawn, leaving our sky, takes the sun along to other people, I turn my crying into joyful singing.

Thus I change the sad tears into joyful singing and mournful accents into sweet tones. Thus, as an animal that scorns the sun enjoys the shade in the solitary woods, I long and desire only that the dawn would never, by bringing in the day, chase night away.

In answer to my languor, my lady appeared one night in a dream and with her hand dried the tears that these eyes were shedding day and night. And in clear tones she said, "There may well be a time when you will no longer be a citizen of the forest," and then she fled like a shadow before the sun.)

Translation by Adriana Slaniceanu.

No. 32—Unidentified, Ballata

32. Se dove è 'l sol che sol te flora alluma,
Ne si sente calore,
Ond'è che qui l'ardore
È tal che tutti quanti ne consuma.
E perchè il sol vinto da più bel sole,
Li suoi concenti rai,
Per volermi dar guai,
Ver' me rivolge e non ver' l'altro sole.
Con dir che l'opra è tale
Ch'un più bel sol vi sia,
Del qual s'hor per mia colpa ne son priva,
Non mi deggio doler s'in fuoco io viva.

(Where the sun shines on you alone, my flower, no heat is felt, while here the heat is such that everyone is consumed by it. It is because the sun, vanquished by a more beautiful sun, turns its scorching rays toward me, wanting to give me woe, and not toward the other sun. While saying that the case is so, that a more beau- tiful sun exists, I—if through my own fault am deprived of it—must not lament were I to live in fire.)

Translation by Adriana Slaniceanu.

Notes to the Texts and Translations

1. *Petrarch's Lyric Poems,* trans. and ed. Robert M. Durling (Cambridge, Mass.: Harvard University Press, 1976). The other translations by Durling that are quoted here are taken from the same work. They are reprinted with the permission of the publisher.

2. Lodovico Ariosto, *Orlando furioso,* trans. Guido Waldman (London: Oxford University Press, 1974). The translation of No. 11 is taken from the same work. The translations are reprinted with the permission of the publisher.

3. The poem describes a battle between Castità (chastity), represented by Diana and her nymphs, and Amore.

4. Rossetti's text in lines 10–11 differs from the accepted text, which reads: *I' pur spero mercè, quantunche tardi, che, ben ella si mostre acerba e fera.* Durling (p. 594) translates: "I still hope for mercy, however late, for, though she show herself bitter and fierce. . . ." In line 9, Rossetti's text substitutes *perchè* for *di che* but without a substantive change in meaning.

CANTO

IL PRIMO LIBRO

DE' MADRIGALI A SEI VOCI

COMPOSTI NVOVAMENTE

DA LO ECCELLENTE MVSICO

Messer Stefano Rossetto, E. S.

IN VINETIA.

Appresso Claudio da Correggio, & Fausto Bethanio Compagni.

M D L X V I.

Plate I. Stefano Rossetti, *Il primo libro de' madrigali a sei voci*, title page.
(Courtesy British Library)

ALLA ILLVSTRISSIMA ET ECCELLENTISSIMA

SIGNORA ET PADRONA MIA OSSERVANDISSIMA

La Signora Donna Isabella de Medici Orsina.

E Cortesi demostrationi che. V. Eccellen. per sua natural bontà vsa verso tutti i virtuosi, e li molti fauori che ella fa ordinariamente alli Amoreuoli suoi, m'ha fatto tener per fermo, che ella habbia fin hora banto ingrado, l'osseruanza & seruitù mia verso di lei qualche ella sia statta; & volendo adesso Mandar in luce alcuni miei Madrigali m'è parso mio debito dedicarli A. V. Eccellen. a cio in vn medesmo tempo essi s'illustrino con la grandezza del suo nome, & a quella faccino testimonio del fedele, & pronto animo mio verso di lei. Prego. V. Eccellen. ad accettarli con quella benignità che la suol fare le cose ben che minime de suoi piu cari seruitori, & mi tenga in sua buona gratia allaquale humilmente mi raccomando, che, N. S. Dio la feliciti.   Da Fiorenza il Dì XXII Maggio MDLXVI.

Di. V. Eccellen.

Hum. Ser.

Stefano Rossetto.

Plate II. Stefano Rossetti, *Il primo libro de' madrigali a sei voci*, dedication page.
(Courtesy British Library)

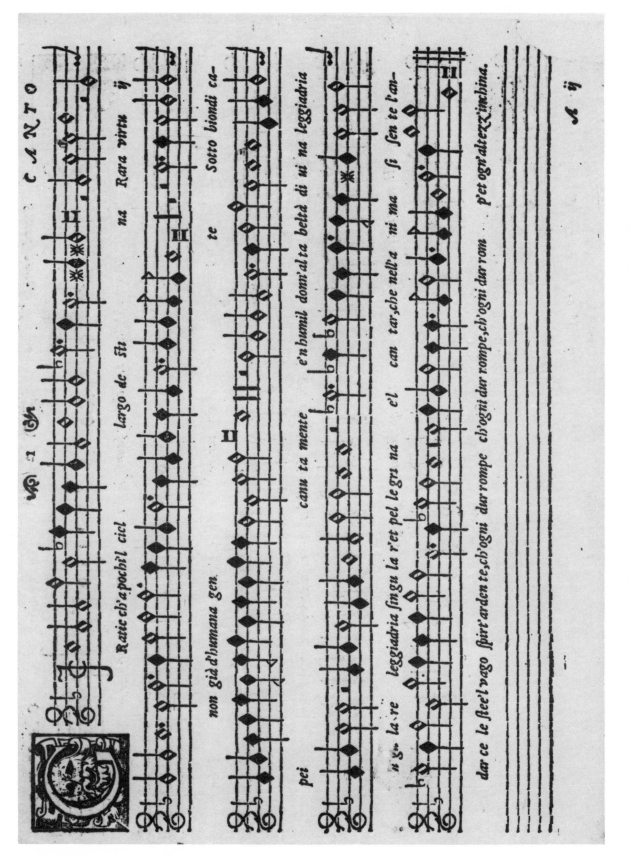

Plate III. Stefano Rossetti, *Gratie ch'a pochi*, canto part, from *Il primo libro de' madrigali a sei voci*. (Courtesy British Library)

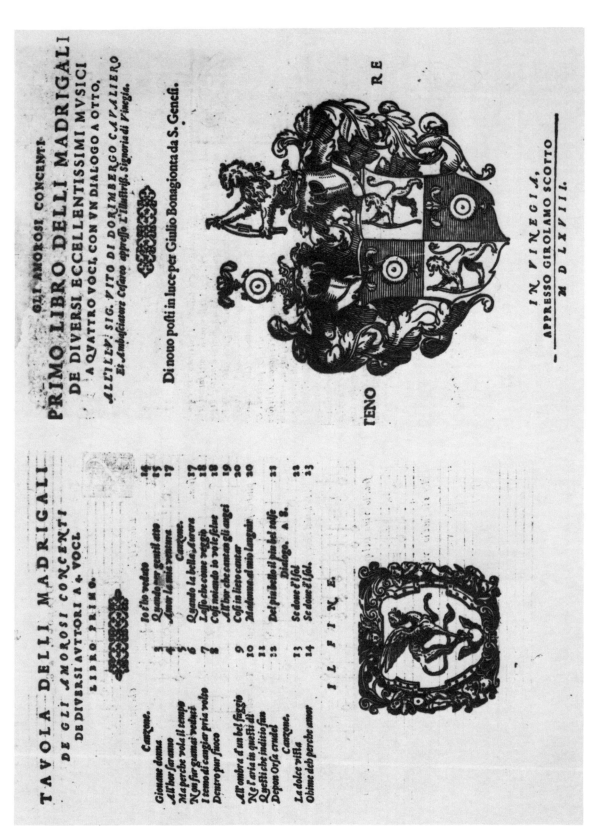

Plate IV. *Gli amorosi concenti primo libro delli madrigali de diversi eccellentissimi musici,*
contents and title page.
(Courtesy Henry E. Huntington Library, San Marino, California)

MADRIGALS
FOR THREE
TO EIGHT VOICES

1. Gratie ch'a pochi

⟨ra- ra vir- tù,⟩ non già d'hu-ma-na gen-

non già d'hu- ma-na gen- te, non già d'hu-

-ra vir- tù,⟩ non già d'hu-ma- - na gen- - te, non

Ra- ra vir- tù, non già d'hu- ma- na gen-te, non già

già d'hu- ma- na gen- - te, non già d'hu- ma- na

ra- ra vir- tù, non già d'hu-

- - te,

-ma- na gen- te, Sot- - to bion- di ca-

già d'hu- ma- na gen- te, Sot- to bion- di ca- pei

d'hu- ma- na gen- te, Sot- to bion- di ca- pei ca-

gen- te, Sot- - to bion- di ca- pei

- ma- na gen- te, Sot- to bion- di ca- pei ca-

4

2. Et quei begli occhi

Petrarch

3. Rotta è l'alta colonna

14

4. Ma se consentimento

Petrarch

Seconda parte

Canto: Ma se con-sen-ti-men- -t'è di de- sti- no, Che

Alto: Ma se con-sen-ti-men- -t'è di de- sti- no, Che

Tenore: Ma se con-sen-ti-men- -t'è di de- sti- no, Che

Quinto: Ma se con- sen- ti- men- -t'è di de- sti - no,

Sesto: Che pos- s'io

Basso: Che pos- s'io

pos- s'io più se no ha-ver l'al-ma tri- sta, Hu- mi-di gl'oc- chi sem-pr'e 'l

pos- s'io più se no ha- - ver l'al- ma tri- sta, Hu- mi-di gl'oc- chi sem-pr'e 'l

pos- s'io più se no ha-ver l'al- ma tri- sta, Hu- mi-di gl'oc- chi sem-pr'e 'l

Che pos- s'io più se no ha-ver l'al- ma tri- sta,

più

Hu- mi-di gl'oc- chi sem-pr'e 'l

più se no ha-ver l'al-ma tri- sta,

5. Come va 'l mondo!

24

sie- de in cie- - l'e'n ter- ra gia- ce!

-la ch'or sie-de in cie- - l'e'n ter- ra gia- ce!

- l'e'n ter- ra gia- ce!

gia- - ce, e'n ter- ra gia- ce!

quel- la ch'or sie-de in cie- l'e'n ter- ra gia- ce!

- de in cie- - l'e'n ter- ra gia- ce!

6. Ma 'l cieco Amor

Seconda parte

Canto

Alto — Ma'l cie-c'A- mor e la mia sor-da men-te, ⟨Ma'l cie- c'A- mor e la_

Quinto — Ma'l cie-c'A- mor e la mia sor-da men-te, ⟨Ma'l cie-c'A-mor e la___

Tenore — Ma'l cie-c'A- mor e la mia sor-da men-te, ⟨Ma'l cie- c'A- mor e la_

Sesto — Ma'l cie-c'A- mor e la mia sor-da men-te, ⟨Ma'l cie- - c'A-mor e la mia sor-da

Basso — Ma'l cie- c'A- mor e la_

Ma'l cie- c'A- mor e la_

30

32

7. Son questi quei begli occhi

[Prima parte]

Son que-sti quei be-gli oc- chi, ⟨son que-sti quei be- gli oc-

Son que-sti quei be-gli oc- chi, ⟨son que-sti quei be-gli oc- chi⟩

Son que-sti quei be-gli oc- chi, ⟨son que-sti quei be- gli oc-

Son que-sti quei be-gli oc- chi, ⟨son que-sti quei be- gli oc-

Son que-sti quei be- gli oc-

Son que-sti quei be- gli oc-

- chi⟩ in cui____ mi- ran- do Sen- za dif- fe- sa

in cui mi- ran- do Sen- za dif- fe- sa far per-

- chi.⟩

- chi⟩ in cui____ mi- ran- do Sen- za dif- fe- sa far____

- chi in cui mi- ran- do Sen- za dif- fe- sa far per- dei me stes-

- chi.

36

38

8. Ahi! Chi sarà colui

40

fi- di Di fè di don- na mo- - bi-l'e in-con- stan- te? E chi più a fem-mi-

fi- di Di fè di don- na mo- - bi-l'e in-con- stan- te? E chi più a

- di Di fè di don- na mo- bi-l'e in-con-stan- - te?

fi- di Di fè di don- na mo- bi- l'e in-con-stan- - te? E chi più a

fi- di Di fè di don- na

fi- di Di fè di don- - na mo- bi- l'e in- - con-stan- te?

- nil pian- to_____ mai cre- - da?

fem-mi-nil pian- to mai cre- da?

E chi più a fem-mi- nil pian-

fem-mi-nil pian- to mai cre- da?

E chi più a fem-mi- nil

E chi più a fem-mi-nil

42

9. Pieno di dolce

10. Se per voi sentì mai

54

11. Io me ne vo la notte

12. Felice me

64

_ l'oc- chio più m'in- vo- glia.

di quel che l'oc- chio più _____ m'in- vo- glia.

_ che l'oc- chio più _____ m'in- vo - glia.

che l'oc- chio più _____ m'in- vo- glia, più m'in- vo- glia.

di quel che l'oc - chio più m'in- vo- glia.

quel che l'oc- chio più _____ m'in- vo- glia.

13. Donna bella e gentil

Canto

[Prima parte]

Quinto

Don- na bel- la e gen- til ch'al ciel pog- gia-

Don- na bel- la e gen- til ch'al ciel pog- gia-

Alto

Don- na bel- la e gen- til ch'al ciel, ___ ch'al ciel ___ pog- gia-

Tenore

Don- na bel- la e gen-

Sesto

Basso

Don- na ___

66

14. Colmo d'ira

72

a par- t'a par- te.

- ro a par- t'a par- te.

- ro a par- - t'a, par- t'a, par- t'a par- te.

spez- zas- se'l car- ro a par- t'a par- te, a par- t'a par- te.

par- te, a par- t'a, par- t'a, par- - t'a par- te.

- ro a par- - t'a, par- t'a, par- t'a par- te.

15. I dolci basci

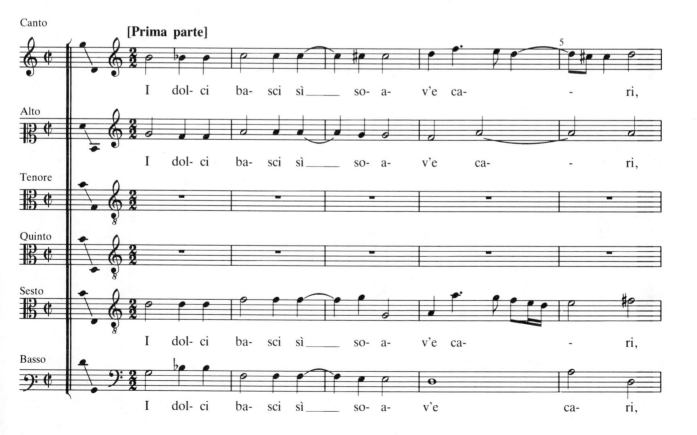

Canto

[Prima parte]

I dol- ci ba- sci sì____ so- a- v'e ca- - ri,

Alto

I dol- ci ba- sci sì____ so- a- v'e ca- - ri,

Tenore

Quinto

Sesto

I dol- ci ba- sci sì____ so- a- v'e ca- - ri,

Basso

I dol- ci ba- sci sì____ so- a- v'e ca- ri,

- c'ac- co- glien- z'e_i dol- c'ac- cen- ti Con

- z'e_i dol- c'ac- cen- ti Con dol-

E le dol- c'ac- co- glien- z'e_i dol- c'ac-cen- ti Con dol- ci

e_i dol-c'ac-cen- ti Con dol- ci

e le dol- c'ac- co- glien- z'e_i dol- c'ac- cen- ti

- glien- z'e_i dol- c'ac- cen- ti

dol- ci mo- d'es- pres- s'u- ni-ch'e ra- ri.

- ci mo- d'es-pres- s'u- ni- ch'e ra- ri, Con

mo-d'es-pres- s'u- ni-ch'e ra- ri, Con dol ci mo- d'es-

mo- d'es- pres-s'u- ni-ch'e ra- ri, Con dol-ci mo- d'es-

Con dol- ci mo- d'es-pres-s'u- ni- ch'e ra-

Con dol- ci mo-d'es- pres-s'u- ni-ch'e

16. M'hanno condotto

84

17. Alla caccia!

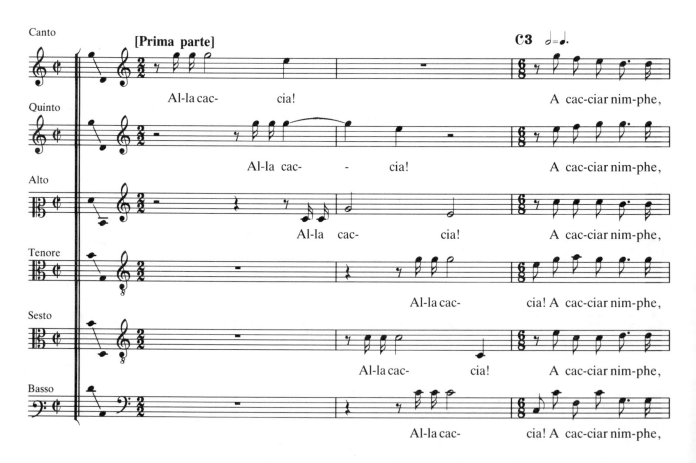

-ze sien di tem- pra du- ra, Ri- - gi- do- se ru-

-ze sien di tem- pra du- ra, Ri- gi- do- se ru-gen- do

sien di tem-pra du- ra, Ri- gi- do- se ru-gen-

-ze sien di tem- pra du- ra, Ri- gi- do- se ru- gen-

-ze sien di tem-pra du- ra, Ri-

-ze sien di tem- pra du- ra, Ri- gi-

-gen- do in- scie- m'u- ni- te.

in- scie- m',in- scie- m'u- ni- te.

-do, ru-gen- d'in- scie- m'u- ni- te. Di

-do, ru- gen- d'in- -scie- m'u-ni- te.

-gi- do- se ru- gen- d'in- scie- me. Di fuo-

-do- se ru-gen- d'in- scie- m'u- ni- te.

-u- ra, ⟨Noi nim-phe ni-chi-lar e far____ pa-u- ra⟩

-u- ra, ⟨Noi nim-phe ni-chi-lar e far____ pa-u- ra⟩

-u- ra, ⟨Noi nim-phe ni-chi-lar e far____ pa-u- ra⟩

nim-phe ni-chi-lar e far pa- u- ra, e far pa-u- ra

_ pa- u- ra, ⟨Noi nim-phe ni-chi-lar____ e far pa-u- ra⟩

-u- ra, ⟨Noi nim-phe ni-chi-lar____ e far____ pa-u- ra⟩

C3

Ap- por-tan-do-cia noi l'an-ti-ca li- te, Ap-por-tan-do-cia noi l'an-ti-ca li- te.

Ap-por-tan- do-cia noi l'an-ti-ca li- te, Ap-por-tan- do-cia noi l'an-ti-ca li- te.

Ap- por-tan-do- cia noi l'an-ti- ca li- te, Ap-por-tan-do- cia noi l'an-ti-ca li- te.

Ap-por- tan- do-cia noi l'an-ti-ca li- te, Ap-por- tan- do-cia noi l'an-ti- ca li- te.

Ap- por-tan-do-cia noi l'an-ti-ca li- te, Ap-por-tan-do-cia noi l'an-ti-ca li- te.

Ap- por-tan- do-cia noi l'an-ti-ca li- te, Ap-por-tan- do-cia noi l'an-ti-ca li- te.

18. Noia non vi serà

- v'in bat- ta- glia̲e ben_____ ar- di- te, Er- ran- d'an-da- te per di qui pro-ter-

- ta- glia̲e ben ar- di - te, Er- ran- d'an-da- te per di qui pro-ter-

- glia̲e ben ar- di - te, Er- ran- d'an-da- te per di qui pro-ter-

- glia̲e ben ar- di - te, Er- ran- d'an-da- te per di qui pro-ter-

- te- te-v'in bat-ta-glia̲e ben ar- di - te, Er- ran- d'an-da- te per di qui pro-ter-

- ta- glia̲e ben_____ ar- di - te, Er- ran- d'an-da- te per di qui pro-ter-

- ve,

- ve, De-si- de- ro- se di far- lo pri-gio- ne,

- ve, De-si- de- ro- se di far- lo pri-gio- ne, ⟨De- si- de- ro- se di far- lo pri-gio-

- ve, De-si- de- ro- se di far- lo pri-gio- ne, ⟨De- si- de- ro- se di far- lo pri-gio-

- ve, De-si- de- ro- se di far- lo pri-gio- ne, ⟨De- si- de- ro- se di far- lo pri-gio-

- ve, De- si- de- ro- se di far- lo pri-gio-

19. Altro non è il mio amor

98

20. S'io potessi mirar

106

la mia fe- ra stel-   la,   ⟨Et____ la mia fe- ra   stel-   la⟩ Del-

la mia fe- ra stel- la _____   Del-

la mia fe- ra stel- la,   Et   la   mia fe- ra stel- la   Del-

la mia fe- ra stel-   - la,   Et   la   mia fe-   - ra stel-   la Del-la mia

Et_____ la mia fe- ra stel-   - la

Et la_____ mia fe- ra   stel-   - la Del-

- la mia don- na bel-   la, _____ ⟨Del- la mia don-   na bel-   - la⟩ M'al-

- la mia don- na bel-   la,   ⟨Del-la   mia don-   na bel- la⟩ M'al-

- la mia don- na bel- la, ⟨Del- la mia don- na bel-   la⟩   M'al-   lon-

don- na bel-   la,   Del- la mia don- na   bel- - la

Del- la   mia don-   na,   del- la mia don- na bel- la

- la mia don- na bel- la, Del- la mia don- na bel-   la

21. È questo 'l nido

116

22. Et m'hai lasciato

118

120

- ti- mo vo - lo, l'ul-

⟨on- de pren- de- st'al ciel⟩ [l'ul- ti- mo vo- lo]

- lo, l'ul- ti-

On-de pren- de- st'al ciel l'ul- ti- mo

- de pren- de-st'al ciel l'ul- ti-mo vo -

on- de pren- de- st'al ciel l'ul- ti- mo vo-

- ti- mo vo - lo Et do- ve gl'oc-

Et do- ve gl'oc- chi tuoi __

- mo vo - lo

vo - lo Et do- ve gl'oc- chi

- lo Et do- ve gl'oc-chi tuoi _____ so-

- lo

23. Nova bellezza

124

24. Nessun visse

-do'l do- lor, _____ dop- pia _____ lo sti- - le,

-do'l do- lor, dop- - pia lo sti- le, _____

-do'l do- lor, dop- pia lo sti- - le, _____

-do'l do- lor, dop- pia lo sti- - le, _____

Che

Che trahe del cor sì la- - cri- mo- - se ri-

Che

Che trahe del cor _____ sì la- cri- mo- se _____ ri- me,

trahe del cor sì _____ la- cri- mo- se ri- -

Che trahe del cor sì la- cri- mo- se ri-

132

25. Quando 'l sol bagna

138

26. Il sonno è 'n bando

Petrarch

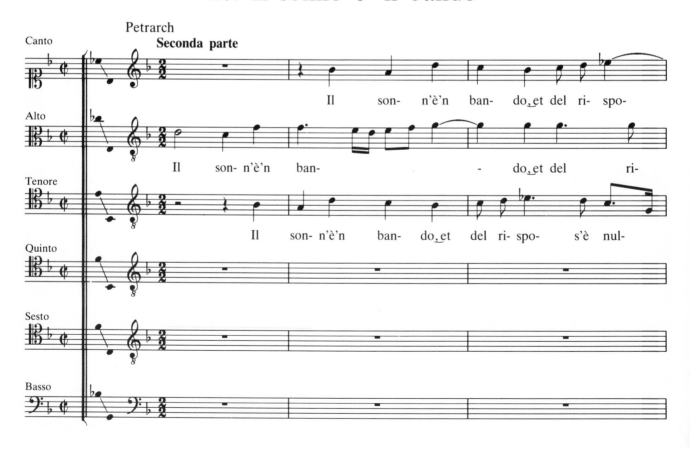

27. La pianta che tanti anni

150

28. Ma, ecco in questa dolce

154

156

29. Au joli bois

162

[30.] S'io non v'amo et adoro

Seconda stanza

Terza stanza

Se quan-do voi ta-l'ho- - ra Ver' me vol-ge- te, in cor-te-

Se quan- do voi ta- l'ho- - ra Ver' me vol-ge- te, in _

Se quan- do voi ta- l'ho- - ra Ver' me vol-ge- te, in _

- s'at- t'e pi- - o, Gl'oc- chi, o sia a ca- so, o che di me vi do-

_ cor-te-s'at- t'e pi- - o, Gl'oc- chi, o sia a ca-so, o che di me _ vi do-

_ cor-te- s'at- t'e pi- - o, Gl'oc- chi, o sia a ca- so, o che di me vi do-

- glia, In fron- t'o-gni sua vo- glia Il cor vi sco-pr'e, _ il cor vi sco-

- glia, In fron- t'o-gni sua vo- glia Il cor vi sco- pr'e, ⟨il cor vi sco-pr'e⟩

- glia, In fron- t'o- gni _ sua vo- glia Il cor vi sco-pr'e vi _

Quarta stanza

Il bel ch'in voi ri- splen-de Non è tal, ___ o mio sol, che sol si bra- mi; Men-tre l'oc-

Il bel ch'in voi ri- splen- de Non è tal, ___ o mio sol, che sol si bra- mi; Men-tre l'oc-

Il bel ch'in voi ri- splen-de Non è tal, o mio sol, che sol si bra- mi; Men-tre l'oc-

-chio vi scor-ge e poi s'o- bli- a Nè d'hu-om che vo-stro sia A- mor tal cu- ra e co-

-chio vi scor-ge e poi s'o- bli- a Nè d'hu-om che vo-stro sia A-mor tal cu- ra e co-

-chio vi scor- ge e poi s'o- bli- a Nè d'hu-om che vo-stro sia A- mor tal cu- ra e co-

- sì po- ca pren-de Che lo la- sc'in po- ter per- ch'u- n'al- tr'a- mi.

- sì po- ca pren- de Che lo la- sc'in po- ter per- ch'u- n'al- tr'a- mi.

- sì po- ca pren- de Che lo la- sc'in po- ter per- ch'u- n'al- tr'a- mi.

174

176

Sesta stanza

- rio a lei la vi- - ta.

- - rio a lei____ la vi- ta.

-pe- rio a lei la vi- - ta.

Settima & ultima stanza

Io cre- do che ba- star____ tu deb- bi so- la, ⟨Io _

Io cre- do che ba- star tu deb- bi so- la,

Io cre- do che____ ba- star tu deb- bi so-

Io cre- do che ba-

_ cre- do che____ ba- star tu deb- bi so- la,⟩ Io cre- do che ba- star tu

⟨Io cre- do che ba- star____ tu deb- bi so- la,⟩

- la, ⟨Io cre- do che ba- star____ tu deb- bi

-star tu deb- bi so- la, ⟨Io cre- do che ba- star tu deb- - bi so-

-po, ⟨nè mi sia huo- - -

se- gua, ⟨Nè mi sia huo-

-n'al- tra ne se- gua,

nè mi sia huo- po ch'u- n'al-

-po,⟩ nè mi sia huo-po ch'u- n'al- tra ne se-

-po ch'u- n'al- tra ne se- gua,⟩ Nè

⟨Nè mi sia huo- -po ch'u-n'al- tra ne

- tra ne se- gua, ⟨Nè _

- gua, ch'u- n'al- -tra ne se- gua.

mi sia huo- po ch'u- n'al- -tra ne se- gua.

se- gua.⟩

_ mi sia huo- po ch'u- n'al- tra ne se- gua.⟩

[31.] Quando la bella aurora

-lo- ro- so pian - - to Tal che fo ri- sen- tir,

-lo- ro- so pian - - to Tal che fo ri- sen- tir,_____ tal

-ro- so pian - - to Tal che fo ri- sen-

do- lo- ro- so pian - - to Tal che fo ri- sen- tir,

tal che fo ri- sen- tir le sel- v'e i bo- schi.

che fo ri- sen- tir_____ le sel- ve____ e i bo- schi.

- tir, tal che fo ri- sen- tir le sel- ve e i____ bo- schi.

tal che fo ri- sen- tir_____ le sel- v'e i bo- schi.

Terza stanza

Co- sì_____ noi- an- d'io vo le sel- v'e i bo-schi E di-

Co- sì noi- an- d'io vo le sel- v'e i bo-schi E__

Co- sì noi- an- d'io vo le sel- v'e i bo-schi E di- c':"In- vi- dio-

Co- sì noi- an- d'io vo le sel- v'e i bo-schi E di-

192

Quarta stanza

Sesta & ultima stanza

Ma-don- n',al mio lan- guir ven- ne u-na not-

Ma-don- n',al mio lan-guir ven- ne u- na not-

Ma- don- n',al mio lan- guir ven- ne u- na not-

Ma- don- n',al mio lan- guir ven- ne u-na not-

-te In so- gn'e con la ma- n'a- -sciu-gò'l pian- - to Che

-te In so- gn'e con la ma- n'a-sciu-gò'l pian- - to Che

-te In so-gn'e con la ma- n'a- - sciu-gò'l pian- - to

-te In so- gn'e con la ma- n'a- sciu- gò'l pian- - to

- ver-sa- van que- st'oc- ch'a not-t'e ad al- ba.

- ver-sa- van que-st'oc- chi a not-t'e ad al- ba.

Che ver-sa- van que-st'oc- ch'a not-t'e ad al- ba. E dis-

E dis-

[32.] Se dove è 'l sol

206